Amy Wild, Animal Talker

The Lost Treasure

Diana Kimpton

Illustrated by
Desideria Guicciardini

USBORNE

The Clamerkin Clan

Hilton

Amy

Einstein

Plato

Isambard

Willow

Bun

To John,
who told me about Roman rings

First published in the UK in 2010 by Usborne Publishing Ltd., Usborne House, 83-85 Saffron Hill, London EC1N 8RT, England. www.usborne.com

Text copyright © Diana Kimpton, 2010

Illustrations copyright © Usborne Publishing Ltd., 2010

The right of Diana Kimpton to be identified as the author of this work has been asserted by her in accordance with the Copyright, Designs and Patents Act, 1988.

Cover photograph © NHPA/Photoshot

The name Usborne and the devices ♀⊕ are Trade Marks of Usborne Publishing Ltd.

This is a work of fiction. The characters, incidents, and dialogues are products of the author's imagination and are not to be construed as real. Any resemblance to actual events or persons, living or dead, is entirely coincidental.

A CIP catalogue record for this book is available from the British Library.

First published in America in 2014 AE.

PB ISBN 9780794529246 ALB ISBN 9781601303196

JFMAMJJASO D/13   02360/2

Printed in Dongguan, Guangdong, China.

CHAPTER ONE

"Which one should I take?" asked Amy Wild, as she stared at the three objects on her bed. There was a black and white photo, a tattered teddy bear and a medal painted to look like silver.

Hilton, the cairn terrier, jumped onto her quilt and pushed the bear with his paw. "Take this," he barked. "It's got the most interesting smell."

"That's not important," squawked
the parrot perched on the windowsill.
"Amy's teacher wants the class to take
in things that are old."

"This bear is old, Plato," said Hilton. "It's got bald patches and one of its ears is wobbly."

Amy wasn't surprised that she could understand what the dog and the parrot were saying. The string of golden paws she wore around her neck was magic – it let her talk to animals. She looked at the bear and smiled. "Maybe I should take that. It was Mom's when she was small."

"I think the medal's more interesting," said Plato. "Did one of your ancestors get it for being a hero?"

Amy laughed. "No. Dad got it for playing football at school."

Hilton peered at the black and white

photo. "I recognize that place. It's your school."

"But it was taken a long time ago," said Amy. "That's Granty's class photo from when she was my age."

"Wow!" said Plato, as he flew onto the bed for a closer look. "That really is old. Which one is she?"

"The girl in the middle," said Amy, as she pointed her out. "Look – she's wearing my necklace." It was Granty, her great-aunt, who had given her the necklace of paws when Amy first moved to Clamerkin Island. And Granty was the only other human in the world who knew about its secret magic.

At that moment, Dad shouted up the stairs, "Hurry up or you'll be late!"

"Coming," yelled Amy. She glanced once more at the three objects. Then she made up her mind, grabbed the photo and raced downstairs.

The hall was empty. So she pushed open the swing door that separated the public and private parts of her home and ran into the Primrose Tea Room. Dad was there. So were Mom and Granty. They were busy spreading clean yellow cloths on the tables, ready for their first customers. But they all stopped to see Amy off to school.

"Here's your lunch," said Dad, pushing a box into her hand.

"I've put in some of my banana cake," said Granty. "I know that's your favorite."

"Look at the time," said Mom. "You'd better hurry or you'll be late."

Amy glanced at the clock and realized Mom was right. She'd taken too long deciding what to take with her. Now she'd have to hurry to get to school on time.

"Bye!" she shouted as she ran out of the Primrose. She raced down the cobbled street and turned onto a narrow, twisty lane with hedges on either side. To her dismay, it was deserted. All the other children were already at school. She could hear them on the playground.

She started to run faster. But she'd only gone a few steps when a flash of black and white feathers dived out of the sky. The magpie flew so close to her face that she felt the tip of its wing brush her nose.

The bird landed on the ground just in front of Amy. She dropped the object she was carrying in her beak, and cried, "Help me!"

Amy stopped. She couldn't resist a request like that, however late it made her. And being late was good in one way – it meant there was no one around who might hear her talking to the magpie. She had to be careful. She had promised Granty she would always keep her special power secret.

"What's wrong, Joy?" she asked as she bent down beside the bird. "I hope you haven't been stealing again."

Joy hopped nervously from foot to foot. "I hope I haven't too. I've been really careful since you told me it was wrong. I never take shiny things from human houses anymore, however much I like them."

"So what's the problem?" asked

Amy, stroking the soft feathers on the magpie's head.

"This is," Joy replied, as she poked the object in front of her with her beak. "I picked it off the ground when I saw it glint in the sunlight. But now I'm worried. It looks too much like one of those ring things that humans wear."

Amy lifted it carefully and laid it on the palm of her hand. The magpie was right – it was a ring. But it was bent and dirty. The stone that decorated it was covered with dirt. It must be a long time since anyone had worn it.

She cleaned the stone on her sleeve and examined it again. This time she noticed there was a picture of a man's head engraved on it. He had a circle of leaves balanced on his hair that reminded Amy of a photo she had seen in a history book.

Joy turned her head to the side and looked into Amy's eyes. "Was I right to bring it to you?" she asked.

"Definitely," said Amy, with what she hoped was a reassuring smile. "It's best if you don't keep human things."

"What will you do with it?" asked Joy.

"I'm not sure," Amy replied, as the bell rang out from the playground. "I'll have to think about it later. If I don't get to school soon, I'll be in trouble." Then she thrust the ring deep into her pocket and started to run.

CHAPTER TWO

By the time Amy reached the playground, everyone had already gone inside. She raced after them and reached her classroom just as her teacher was calling the last name on the roll. Luckily that name was Amy's.

"Here!" she called as she ran through the door.

Mrs. Damson raised her eyebrows in disapproval. "You're just in time. Now settle down quickly. I want to see what everyone has brought for history."

"So do I," purred Einstein, the school cat, as he sat down beside Amy's chair. "What have you brought?"

Amy reached down and stroked the white Persian's fluffy fur. "A photo," she whispered so quietly that only he could hear. Her ability to talk to animals was a secret she mustn't share.

One by one, the children came to the front of the class to show their pieces of history. Veronica's doll with a china face had belonged to her great-grandmother while Luke's great-uncle had once played with his battered lead soldier. The twins, Jade and Josie Tink, both brought gadgets from the days before electricity. Jade's was an iron that had to be heated up on the stove, while Josie's was designed for putting out candles.

Amy was glad she'd decided to bring the photo. It was a real piece of Island history, and she was sure everyone would love it. She held it carefully on her lap where only Einstein could see. There was just Nathan left. Then it would be her turn.

Nathan stood up and swaggered to the front of the class. "I've got the best thing ever," he boasted. He waved his hand toward the other objects laid out on the history table and sneered, "Mine's much better than all that junk."

"There's no need to be unpleasant," scolded Mrs. Damson. "It's not a competition."

"Trust Nathan to be rude," muttered Einstein.

Amy nodded in agreement. School would be much more fun without Nathan and his bullying ways.

He didn't bother to apologize to the teacher. He just opened his school bag and pulled out a photograph. "This was taken on the playground years and years ago. That's my granddad at the end of the line."

Amy stared at his picture in dismay. It was exactly the same as the one she was holding.

Everyone loved Nathan's photo just as much as she had hoped they would like hers. They passed it eagerly from hand to hand, trying to pick out their own relatives from the group of children in the picture. Only Amy didn't need to – she already knew which one was Granty.

She slumped miserably in her chair. "I wish I'd chosen something else," she muttered, half to herself and half to Einstein.

"I'm sure it doesn't matter that yours is the same," purred the white cat.

Amy was sure that it did. She was going to be the only person in the whole class who couldn't show something that no one had seen before. When Mrs. Damson called her name, she walked unwillingly to the front of the class, clutching her copy of the photo.

Nathan snickered as she passed his desk and he saw what she was carrying. "Copycat!" he jeered. Then he smiled sneekily and added, "I've really messed up your presentation, haven't I?"

"No, you haven't," said Amy, trying hard not to show Nathan she was upset. She reached the front and turned to face the class. As she looked at their expectant faces, she thought longingly of the teddy bear and the medal lying on her bed at home. If only she'd brought them with her. Then she'd have something else to show instead of the photo.

Suddenly she remembered her meeting with the magpie, and that gave her an idea. She pushed her hand into her pocket and pulled out the ring. "I've brought this," she announced, as she held it up for everyone to see. "I think it's very, very old. There's a picture on it of a man who looks like a Roman."

There was a moment of stunned silence. Then Luke bounded to his feet and yelled, "It's Roman."

Jade and Josie Tink glanced at each other and squealed with excitement. "Marcus Fabricus," they cried in unison. Their words rippled around the room as the other children repeated them.

Amy watched in confusion. What were they all talking about?

Eventually Mrs. Damson clapped her hands for silence. "Calm down, all of you. This might not mean what you're all thinking." Then she looked at Amy and asked in a serious voice. "Where did you get that ring? Did you bring it with you when you moved here from the city?"

"No," replied Amy. She hesitated for a moment, wondering how much of the truth she could share without revealing her secret. It seemed safest not to mention the magpie, so she just said, "I found it on the ground on my way to school. It's definitely an Island ring."

Her words caused another buzz of

excitement in the room. And that made her feel more confused than ever. "I don't understand," she said. "Why is everyone so worked up about the ring?"

"Because it might prove the historians wrong," explained Mrs. Damson. "The ones who say the Romans never came to the Island. And if it's true that the Romans were here, the tale of the lost Roman treasure might be true too."

Now it was Amy's turn to feel excited. Could there really be treasure hidden somewhere on Clamerkin Island? And had she found a vital clue?

CHAPTER THREE

"Let me have the ring," said Mrs. Damson, as the bell sounded for break. "I'll show it to some experts to see what they think."

Amy was happy to hand it over. She didn't want the responsibility of looking after something that might be so important. It would be dreadful if anything happened to it now.

Out on the playground, she quickly found Jade and Josie Tink. "Who's this Marcus Fabricus?" she asked.

The twins stared at her in surprise. "Do you really not know?" asked Jade.

"Of course I don't," said Amy. "I wouldn't be asking if I did."

Unfortunately Nathan overheard. "Trust you to be stupid," he taunted. "Have you forgotten the story Mrs. Damson taught us last summer?"

Amy put her hands on her hips and glared at him. "You're the brainless one, not me. You've forgotten that I just moved to Clamerkin this year."

The twins giggled. "She's right," said Jade.

"You're definitely brainless," said Josie.

Nathan's face turned red with anger. But he didn't say any more. He just spun on his heel and stomped away.

Amy waited until he was out of earshot. Then she turned back to Jade and Josie. "Come on. Tell me about Marcus Fabricus."

"He was a very important Roman," said Jade.

"Was the treasure his?" Amy asked.

Josie nodded. "The story says he was taking it back to Rome when his ship was damaged in a storm. The sailors landed on Clamerkin Island and managed to repair the ship. But it wasn't strong enough to carry all the cargo – they had to lighten the load."

"Gold's really heavy," said Jade. "So Marcus Fabricus buried all his treasure somewhere on the Island, and the story says it's still here. He never came back for it."

"Wow!" said Amy. "No wonder everyone's so excited."

But that excitement had to be put

aside for the rest of the morning. Mrs. Damson insisted on lessons as usual. Then halfway through the lunch break, she called Amy in from the playground. "Come with me. Someone wants to talk to you."

She led the way to the principal's office and ushered Amy inside. Mr. Plimstone was sitting behind his desk, as usual. But he wasn't alone. Two other people were sitting beside him – a chubby man in a well-worn suit and a tall lady holding a notebook and pencil.

Amy felt nervous and outnumbered. She was glad when Einstein slipped through the half-open door and joined her.

"Hello, Amy," said Mr. Plimstone with a warm smile. He waved his hand toward the man. "I expect you know Mr. Jackson."

Amy nodded. "You run the library."

"And I'm president of Clamerkin Historical Society." He carefully lifted the ring out of the box he was holding and laid it on the desk. "Your find has caused great interest, young lady."

"It's fantastic," cried the woman, as she jumped to her feet. She grabbed Amy's hand and shook it vigorously. "I'm Mavis King, freelance reporter. I'm so glad I'm on the Island today. This story could be the one that gets me on TV."

Amy pulled her hand out of Mavis's grasp as politely as she could. Then she asked, "Is the ring really that important?"

"Absolutely," said Mr. Jackson. "It's a Roman intaglio."

"Intagli what?" asked Amy.

"Intaglio," Mr. Jackson repeated. "It's like a modern signet ring. The important Roman who owned it would have pressed the picture on the stone into wax to make his mark."

"Instead of a signature," added Mr. Plimstone.

Mr. Jackson picked up the ring again and stared at it with admiration. "Until today, there's been no proof that the Romans ever came to

Clamerkin. So we've always believed that the story of the treasure wasn't true – that it was just a tale someone made up long ago."

He paused dramatically. For a few seconds, the only sound was Mavis's pencil scritch-scratching across her notebook. Then Amy dared to ask, "Has the ring changed that?"

"Absolutely," said Mr. Jackson. "Now we've found something genuinely Roman on the Island, all things are possible. Maybe the treasure really does exist."

Amy's spine tingled with excitement. "Do you think the ring belonged to Marcus Fabricus?"

"Probably not," said Mr. Jackson. "He would have kept his own intaglio with him. But it could have belonged to someone traveling with him, or it might even be part of the treasure itself."

"What's going to happen next?" asked Mavis King, as she pulled a camera from her bag.

"We need to investigate," said Mr. Jackson. "So we need to know exactly how you found the ring, Amy."

"Careful," mewed Einstein, whisking his tail in warning. He knew about the magpie. Amy had told him at lunchtime.

But Amy already knew she must be cautious. "I found it on the road," she said, sticking to the half-truth she had told in class. That had been good enough for Mrs. Damson, so she hoped it would satisfy everyone here as well.

It didn't. "How did you spot it?" asked Mr. Jackson.

"Was it buried?" asked Mr. Plimstone.

Luckily Mavis chose that moment to start taking photographs. That gave Amy some thinking time before she had to answer.

She didn't have much choice now –
she would have to bring the magpie
into her story. But she needed to do
that without mentioning that Joy
had talked to her. Amy waited until
Mavis had finished. Then she took a
deep breath and said, "The ring was
lying on the ground. I saw a magpie
drop it."

Mr. Plimstone leaned back in his
chair and rubbed his chin thoughtfully.
"That makes sense. Magpies like
glittery things. One might easily have
been attracted to the ring."

"But why would it drop it?" asked
Mavis.

"And how did it find it in the first
place?" added Mr. Plimstone.

"That's the really important question," said Mr. Jackson. "I can see from the dirt on the ring that it was underground until very recently, and I don't think magpies dig."

All three of them looked questioningly at Amy. Amy looked back as confidently as she could. But inside she was starting to panic. She knew she could find the information they wanted by asking Joy where she found the ring. But she didn't want to do that. Answering these questions would just encourage them to ask more. They'd want to know how she'd found out what the magpie had done. And how could she explain that without revealing her secret power?

The treasure didn't seem so exciting anymore. Now it was more of a threat – something that might let the whole world know that the necklace of paws was magic. Amy was desperate to prevent that from happening, but she wasn't sure she could do it by herself.

As she stepped out from Mr. Plimstone's office, she turned to Einstein and said, "Call a clan meeting." Amy was the only human member of the group of animals who looked after Clamerkin Island. Usually the clan solved problems for other animals. But today it was Amy herself who needed help.

CHAPTER FOUR

Mavis King worked quickly. The news of the ring was all over the Island by the time Amy got home from school.

"Isn't it exciting?" said Mom, as Amy stepped into the Primrose Tea Room.

"We've heard all about it on the local radio station," said Dad.

"And I saw it on TV," said Granty.

"Plato was thrilled when he saw a picture of you."

"Funny old bird," said Mom. "It's almost as if he understands what's going on."

Amy resisted the urge to tell her that he did. That would just make the situation worse. Instead, she smiled and said, "I think I'll take Hilton for a walk."

"Keep your eyes open for the treasure while you're out," said Dad, with a laugh.

Amy forced herself to smile. But she didn't have any enthusiasm for treasure hunting. Life would be so much simpler if Joy had never found the ring.

She found Hilton in the living room with Plato. He jumped up when he saw her. "Einstein's organized the meeting," he barked. He was a member of the clan too, and so was Plato.

"I'm not coming this time," said the

parrot from his perch in front of the TV. "The news is too interesting at the moment. There's lots about Clamerkin Island."

Amy wasn't surprised. He loved television so much that he often chose to stay at home. So she left him where he was, got changed and headed out into the garden with Hilton.

When they reached the far end, the terrier dived into a clump of bushes. Amy followed, pushing her way through the branches. Then she stepped into the clearing in the middle that was the clan's almost-secret meeting place. Einstein was already there. So were the other three members of the clan.

Willow, the Siamese cat, pricked up her ears when she saw Amy. "Everyone in the post office is talking about that ring. They all want to find the treasure."

"So does my human," said the tabby cat named Isambard. "He has his metal detector out and is trying to make it work." He gazed wistfully at the sky and added, "Wonderful things, metal detectors. They can help you find the nuts and bolts you've lost."

"Nuts and bolts!" said Bun, the fat black cat from the bakery. "Is that what treasure is? I was hoping it was something I could eat."

Einstein laughed. "Treasure's not food. It's gold and silver and pieces of eight."

"That's pirates' treasure," said Amy, correcting him as gently as she could. "I expect Roman treasure is different."

"Perhaps they have pieces of nine," the Persian cat suggested.

Amy suspected that was wrong too, but she decided not to argue. "I think this treasure is mainly gold. That's why Marcus Fabricus left it behind – gold is very heavy."

"Does it matter what it is?" barked Hilton. "I'm much more interested in why you called this meeting."

"I need your advice," explained Amy. She sat down beside the cats and told them what had really happened that morning – how the magpie had asked her advice and given her the ring. Then she repeated the simpler version she had told everyone else.

"Do you think that's believable?" she asked when she'd finished. "Everyone's sure to keep asking me questions, and

I'm scared that I'll say too much and give away the fact that I can talk to you all. And if I do that, the secret of the necklace won't be secret for much longer."

There was a long pause while everyone thought. Eventually Einstein said, "Your story sounds all right to me."

Isambard nodded his agreement. "When people ask questions, just say you don't know any more."

"For once, I agree with Bun," said Hilton. "I don't understand why humans get so excited about treasure you can't eat."

Willow yawned and washed her paw. "It's just a lot of fuss about nothing. By tomorrow, everyone will have forgotten all about it. Just wait and see."

But the Siamese cat was wrong. The next morning was Thursday – publication day for the *Clamerkin Chronicle*. Thanks to Mavis King, the story of the Roman ring was on the front page of the Island's newspaper, and that triggered a fresh burst of treasure-hunting fever.

Everywhere Amy went, she was bombarded with questions.

"Would you recognize the magpie if you saw it again?" asked Mr. Jackson, the president of the historical society, when he met her on her way to school.

"Which direction did the magpie

come from?" asked Mr. Plimstone when she arrived.

"Where's the treasure?" Nathan demanded at lunchtime.

"I don't know," Amy replied over and over again. It soon became such a habit that she could say it without thinking. She kept hoping the questions would stop. But Mavis King wasn't ready to give up yet.

By Friday morning, the reporter had spread the story of the ring to the mainland newspapers and radio. Now it wasn't just the residents of Clamerkin Island who had gold fever. All day long, streams of treasure hunters poured off the ferry from the mainland, laden with backpacks, maps and shovels.

Soon the usually quiet countryside of Clamerkin Island was alive with people. Some waved metal detectors, some dug holes and others crawled through the grass on their hands and knees.

But all of them were looking for the same thing – the gold Marcus Fabricus had buried centuries before.

Amy didn't join in the search. She wished she had never shown the ring to anyone. Then the treasure hunt would never have happened, and her secret wouldn't be at risk.

CHAPTER FIVE

When Amy arrived home from school on Friday afternoon, she found a line outside the Primrose Tea Room. So many treasure hunters wanted food and drink that all the tables were full.

Amy kept her head down, hoping no one would recognize her and start asking questions. As a result, she didn't look where she was going and almost tripped over Hilton.

"Come quickly," he barked. "There's an urgent clan meeting. Plato's busy keeping up with the TV news, but the cats are already there."

"I'll be as fast as I can," Amy promised. She ran down the path beside the Primrose and threw open the back door.

"What's the rush?" Mom called from the kitchen.

Amy knew she couldn't tell her the truth. So she just said, "I'm in a hurry to take Hilton for a walk. It's such a sunny afternoon."

"It's a really busy one here," said Mom. She looked up from the sandwiches she was making and smiled wearily. "I'll be glad when all these treasure hunters have gone, and we just have our usual customers again."

"So will I," said Amy. When the treasure hunt was over, the questions would stop too.

As soon as she was outside again, Hilton led the way down the garden. But when he reached the end, he didn't head toward the almost-secret meeting place. Instead, he slipped through a gap between the hedge and the shed and disappeared.

Amy squeezed through too and found the terrier waiting for her on the path on the other side. "Where are we going?" she asked. "I thought there was a meeting."

"There is," said Hilton. "But it's not in the usual place. That's all right for cats and dogs, but we'd never get a cow in there."

Amy's mouth dropped open in astonishment. "What cow?"

Hilton was in too much of a hurry to answer. "Come on," he barked, as he ran off up the path.

Amy followed close behind. They skirted around a treasure hunter on her hands and knees, searching a grassy bank. Then they dived through a gateway into a field and raced uphill toward a small group of trees at the top.

On the way, they passed a man and woman wearing matching sweaters and knitted hats. They were carrying matching shovels.

"We're looking for the gold," said the lady.

"Is this a good place to dig?" asked the man.

"I don't know," said Amy, as she always did. The holes dotted around the grass suggested these weren't the first treasure seekers to search this field.

Amy didn't wait to see if they started digging. She just ran on up the hill and followed Hilton into the woods.

"Everyone's on the other side," he barked, as he twisted and turned between the trees.

Amy followed as fast as she could. She had to jump over tree roots and duck to avoid low branches. But eventually she reached the end of the woods and stopped in surprise.

She had never seen so many different types of animals in one place before.

The four cats from the clan were lying in the shade of an old oak. Its branches were crowded with birds – pigeons and sparrows sat side by side with woodpeckers and jackdaws. Joy, the magpie, was there too and an owl who blinked sleepily in the daylight.

The ground in front of the tree was equally crowded. Amy recognized Barney, the border collie. But she hadn't met the squirrels before or the rats or the hedgehogs or the badger.

The cow Hilton had mentioned was standing in the nearby field with her head over the fence. The goat next to her wasn't tall enough to put her head over the top so she'd poked it between the rails instead.

A whole family of rabbits was nibbling the grass between the fence and the cats, as if they hadn't a care in the world. "Why aren't they frightened of him?" Amy asked Hilton, as she pointed at a fox lying under a bush.

"There's a truce," explained the terrier. "He and the owl have promised not to do any hunting before sunset."

"We'd better get started then," said Amy. "It's already late afternoon." She stepped out of the woods onto the

grass, being very careful where she put her feet.

"She's here, Gladys," twittered one of the sparrows to his mate.

Amy waved at him. "Hello, Alf," she called.

The sound of her voice sent most of the baby rabbits scurrying behind their mother. But the boldest stayed where he was and gazed at Amy with wide, brown eyes. "Look, Mom!" he yelled. "The Talker's here, and she really can understand what we say."

"I never doubted for a moment," bleated the goat.

"Yes, you did," said the cow. "You told me so yesterday."

The goat suddenly became very interested in the ground. "I was wrong," she muttered in a voice made squeaky with embarrassment.

"Don't worry," said Amy. "I found it hard to believe myself at first."

"Really?" cried the goat, looking more cheerful.

"I expect she's just being polite," whispered the cow. Then she looked at Amy and said. "I'm Desdemona, by the way."

"And I'm Cleo," added the goat.

All the other animals immediately

followed their lead and started to introduce themselves. The noise was deafening, and Amy struggled to remember which name went with which face.

At the same time, she wondered what the meeting was about. Was it something to do with the treasure hunt? And was it possible for Amy and the rest of the clan to help so many animals at once?

CHAPTER SIX

When the animals had finished introducing themselves, Willow strode forward and took command. "We're here today because so many of you have asked the clan for help. Now that Amy's arrived, you'd better explain what the problem is."

"It's those treasure hunters," said a badger named Finlay. "They're ruining the Island."

"They've dug holes all over our field," said Cleo.

"They've left litter in our lane," said Barney.

"And my babies can't get a wink of sleep," twittered Gladys, fluffing out her feathers crossly.

The mother rabbit nodded sympathetically.

"Neither can mine. It used to be so quiet and safe underground. But it's not anymore. There's too much digging going on."

Joy hung her head. "I wish I'd left that stupid ring exactly where it was. Then none of this would have happened, and life would be just as good as it used to be."

The crowd of animals murmured their agreement. "Can the magic necklace undo what's happened?" asked Finlay the badger. "Can it make everything go back to how it was?"

"I'm sorry," said Amy. "It can't fix this. The necklace only has one magic power, and that's the one that lets me talk to all of you."

There was a long pause. Judging by the many disappointed faces, Finlay wasn't the only animal who had hoped for a magical solution.

It was Desdemona who eventually broke the silence. "How else can we make the treasure hunters stop?" she mooed.

"We could just wait," Bun suggested. "They're sure to lose interest eventually."

"But that might take ages," bleated Cleo. "And we've already got more holes in our field than we can cope with."

"What we need is a distraction," said Willow. "They'd soon lose interest in the treasure if we gave them something else to think about."

The fox gave a sly grin. "I could raid a few hen houses. That usually attracts attention."

Amy gulped. She didn't want any chickens hurt. But she also didn't want to upset the fox – he was just as worried as all the others and he *had* agreed to the truce. So she smiled at him as sweetly as she could and said, "Thank you for your kind offer. But I don't think violence is the answer."

"I could ask all my friends and relatives to raid the carrot field," said Harper, the father rabbit. "That would definitely attract the farmer's attention."

"But not anyone else's," said Isambard. "My human is one of the treasure hunters, and he's not remotely interested in carrots."

Amy looked at him with renewed interest. "What would make him stop searching?"

"Nothing really," replied the tabby cat. "He won't give up until the treasure is found."

"Oh dear," mooed Desdemona. "The situation's hopeless."

"No, it's not," said Amy with a big grin. "Clever old Isambard has found the solution."

The tabby cat sat up proudly. Then he looked slightly confused and asked, "What solution would that be exactly?"

Amy reached over and tickled his ears. "*We've* got to find the treasure.

Once we've done that, everyone will have to stop looking for it."

"That's brilliant," bleated Cleo.

"But very difficult," said Willow. "If all these humans can't find the treasure, why do you think that we can?"

"Because we've got Joy to help us. If she tells us where she found the ring, we'll know where to start looking."

She looked expectantly at the magpie. So did all the other animals.

Joy nodded her head toward the north. "I found it in that field over there, the one next to Desdemona's. It was in the bottom corner by the stream, lying on top of a pile of bare dirt."

"So let's investigate," said Einstein.

"Do we have to do that now?" asked Bun. "My tummy's telling me that it's almost time for dinner."

"So is mine," agreed the fox, in a soft voice that had just a hint of menace. He smiled at the assembled animals, giving them all a perfect view of his sharp, white teeth.

Amy didn't like that smile. It was sneaky – just like Nathan's. The mice, rats and rabbits didn't trust it either. They squeaked with alarm and scurried to safety behind the clan.

Hilton jumped to his feet and faced the fox. "Remember the truce," he growled.

The fox smiled again. "Of course I will." Then he glanced at the sky and added, "But it's not long until sunset."

Amy knew he was right, and she didn't want anyone to get hurt. So she said, "I think we should end the meeting for today. We'll start hunting for the treasure in the morning."

"Who exactly is 'we'?" asked Desdemona. "Only I can't hunt much because I'm not supposed to go out of my field."

"And Alf and I have the babies to take care of," twittered Gladys.

"Don't worry," said Amy. "It'll be best if there aren't many of us. We don't want to attract too much attention."

Isambard nodded his agreement. "Maybe us clan members should go by ourselves."

"We'll need Joy as well," said Willow. "She's got to show us exactly where she found the ring."

"Can I come?" begged the boldest baby rabbit, bouncing up and down with enthusiasm. "Everyone says the treasure's underground, and I'm very good at digging."

"That's true," said his father. "But I'd better come too. My paws are stronger than our Rascal's."

"Okay, Harper," said Amy. "That's settled."

The treasure-hunting team arranged to meet the next morning. Then the smaller animals scurried away, anxious to be home before the truce ended.

The following day, Amy and Hilton set off right after breakfast. Plato stayed at home again, watching the news. He promised to let them know if anyone else found the treasure in the meantime.

The cats caught up with them on the far side of the trees. "This must be the most important thing we've ever done," said Einstein, as they marched across the field next to Desdemona's. "We've never tried to help so many animals at once before."

"I just wish it didn't involve so much walking," puffed Bun, who was struggling to keep up.

"It's your own fault," scolded Isambard. "You shouldn't have asked your human for that extra helping of breakfast."

"I was just playing it safe," said the fat, black cat. "We won't be back in time for my mid-morning snack, and I might miss lunch as well."

At that moment, Rascal bounded up to meet them. "Hurry up," he called. "We're all waiting." Then he turned and ran back the way he'd come.

The others ran after him. Even Bun tried his best until Amy took pity on him and picked him up. "Thanks," he whispered as he snuggled into her arms.

Rascal led the way to the corner of the field where Joy and Harper were waiting beside a small mound of dirt. Amy had expected to see that because the magpie had mentioned it at yesterday's meeting. But she was surprised to see that it wasn't the only mound. The grass around the stream was dotted with so many heaps of bare soil that it looked as if it had chickenpox.

"This is where I found the ring," said Joy, as she hopped onto the nearest mound. She looked around with a worried expression. "Or maybe it was that pile over there. Or the one to the left. Or the one to the right."

Amy felt her stomach knot with nerves. If the magpie couldn't remember where she found the ring, they'd lost their only clue to where the treasure was. How were they going to find it now?

CHAPTER SEVEN

"I don't think we're in the right place," said Isambard. "All this freshly dug dirt probably means the treasure hunters have already searched this area."

"I'm not so sure," barked Hilton. "Although there's been lots of digging, there aren't any holes." He put his nose to the ground and ran around sniffing the heaps of soil. Then he looked up and wagged his tail. "This isn't human work," he announced. "The only animal I can smell on this dirt is mole."

"That must be Webster," said Harper. "He's the only mole in this area."

"Was he at the meeting?" asked Amy. She hadn't noticed a mole there. In fact, she'd never seen a mole anywhere before.

Harper shook his head. "He was too shy to go. He doesn't like crowds – moles never do. But he might come now. I'll go and find him." He hopped away and vanished down a nearby rabbit hole. After a few minutes, he popped up again looking very pleased with himself. "He's on his way."

He had only just finished speaking when the grass in front of Amy began to move. It heaved slightly, then it split open and dirt spilled out. Finally a small nose appeared in the middle of the dirt.

"Am I in the right place?" asked the nose. "I'm looking for the clan."

"That's us," said Willow, the Siamese. "You can come out. It's perfectly safe."

The dirt moved again and the rest of the mole emerged from underground. He was much smaller than Amy had expected. Most of his body was covered with fur that looked like smooth, black velvet. But his front paws were bald and pink and designed for digging.

Webster peered around short-sightedly and snuffled the air. "I can smell human. Is the Talker here?"

"That's me," said Amy. "We've come to ask you for some help."

"I hope you don't need any digging done," grumbled the mole. "I'm run off my feet at the moment, repairing damage to my tunnels. There are too many heavy-footed humans around at the moment, present company excluded of course."

"They're looking for treasure," said Willow. "And you're not the only one they're annoying."

The mole gave a shriek of terror. "Treasure hunters! They must be after my earthworm collection."

"Don't panic," said Isambard.
"Humans don't think earthworms are
treasure."

"Or sardines," said Bun.

"They're only interested in gold,"
explained Einstein.

"But that's no use to anyone," said
Webster. "You can't eat gold – I've
tried. It's much too hard."

Joy flew over and landed in front of
him. "What gold did you try? Was it
a ring?"

The mole thought for a moment.
"Is a ring a circle with a hole in the
middle?"

"Yes, it is!" cried the magpie. Then
she turned her head to the side and
asked, "Did you find one and dump

it on a molehill?"

Webster nodded. "I was delighted to get rid of it. I only wish the other stuff was light enough to move."

"What other stuff?" asked Amy.

"All those gold things that keep getting in my way. I've got great plans for some tunnels by that tree over there, but I can't dig them because of all that garbage."

Amy felt a shiver of excitement run down her back. "That's not garbage," she cried. "I think that's the treasure. Can you show us where it is?"

"I'll be quicker underground," said Webster. He vanished head first into the earth. Then he quickly popped up again beside the tree. "It's just under here," he called.

Amy waved at the baby rabbit. "Come on, Rascal. We need you."

Rascal rushed over and started digging. Harper went and helped. So did Hilton. Soon the air was full of flying dirt thrown up by the terrier's feet.

Joy flew up into the tree for safety while the four cats took refuge under the hedge. Only Amy and the mole stayed where they were.

Webster sighed. "That's the trouble with other animals. None of them can dig as neatly as a mole."

"But you leave molehills everywhere," said Amy.

"And very neat hills they are too," said Webster. "We moles don't go chucking dirt around like dogs do."

At that moment, Rascal gave a shout from underground. "We've hit something hard. Maybe it's the treasure."

"Can you pull it out?" asked Amy.

"No," said Rascal. "It's too smooth and heavy for Dad and me."

"And for me," added Hilton, as the two rabbits and the terrier reversed rapidly out of the hole. "It needs someone bigger and stronger."

"Like the Talker!" Rascal shouted.

Amy lay face down on the loose dirt and reached into the hole. "I can't feel anything," she said, as she wiggled her fingers around. "Are you sure there's something there?"

"Of course I am!" cried Rascal. "You're not far enough in."

Amy pushed her arm even further into the hole. This time her fingers touched something smooth and hard. But she couldn't get hold of it. Somehow she had to get closer.

She dug her feet into the soft ground and pushed herself forward, forcing her shoulder into the hole as well as her arm. This time she managed to get her fingers around the edge of whatever it was they had found. She grabbed hold and pulled it out into the daylight.

"Ooh," shrieked Joy. "It's shiny."

"And it's big," said Einstein, as all the animals crowded together for a better look. "It's much bigger than a ring."

Amy's hands shook with excitement as she brushed the loose dirt off the flat disk she was holding. "I think it's a plate – a *gold* plate."

"I like plates," said Bun. "They often have sardines on them."

"This one doesn't," said Einstein. He walked forward and gave the plate an experimental lick. "Webster's right. You definitely can't eat gold."

"I told you so," said the mole. "That thing's as useless as all the other stuff down there. It's all made of gold."

Amy listened to his words in delight. There was no doubt in her mind now. She jumped to her feet and waved the plate in triumph. "We've found the treasure."

"Yippee!" cried Rascal.

Einstein looked pleased too. "That's another success for the clan. Clamerkin will be peaceful again as soon as you tell everyone where it is."

"He's right," barked Hilton. "Let's go!"

Amy hesitated, looking at the plate she was holding. "I think I'll leave this behind," she said, as she popped it back into the hole. She pushed some dirt over it for protection and added, "It will be safer here — I don't want to drop it on the way and damage it."

"Come on!" barked Hilton. "I can't wait to see everyone's faces when they hear you've found the treasure."

"Neither can I," purred Willow. "They'll be even more excited than when they heard about the ring."

The cat's words brought memories flooding back into Amy's mind. She remembered that awkward conversation in Mr. Plimstone's office — the one where Mavis King and Mr. Jackson had quizzed her about the ring. She remembered all the questioning from other people too.

Amy slumped to the ground and put her head in her hands. "It's no use," she said. "*I* can't tell everyone what I've done. If I do, they'll all ask loads of questions about how I knew where to look, and I don't see how I can answer them without giving away the secret of the necklace."

"You might manage," said Bun.

"But I might *not*. Don't you see? I *can't* tell anyone about the treasure. The risk is too great."

There was a long pause. Eventually Isambard broke the silence. "Maybe it's a risk you have to take."

"I think so too," said Willow. "If you don't, the treasure hunters won't stop. They'll keep digging holes and damaging animals' homes and frightening their babies."

"They're right," said Einstein. "The animals of Clamerkin Island need you to help them. You can't let them down."

Amy looked around at the others. She could tell by their expressions that they all agreed with the three cats. "I suppose I don't have much choice," she said with a sigh. Then she climbed slowly to her feet and set off unwillingly toward the town.

CHAPTER EIGHT

Amy walked slowly, forcing her reluctant feet to keep going. Hilton stayed close beside her while the cats followed at a distance. Joy came too, flying from bush to bush along the way.

Amy felt as if she was being torn in two. On the one hand, she wanted to help all her animal friends by making

Clamerkin Island peaceful again.
On the other, she wanted to keep the
promise she had made to Granty – the
promise not to tell anyone about her
ability to talk to animals.

If she didn't help her friends, they
would all be unhappy. But if she was
forced to reveal the secret, everyone
in the world would find out about the
necklace's magic power. And what
would happen then? Suppose some
grown-ups decided it was too important
for her to keep. Suppose scientists took
it away to study how it worked. Either
way she'd lose the necklace. Then she
wouldn't be able to talk to animals
anymore, and that possibility made her
feel utterly miserable.

Amy glanced across the field and saw some treasure hunters in the distance, damaging the rabbit holes where Rascal and his family lived. Some more were busy digging up the ground around Finlay the badger's home. They really were ruining the animals' lives. Isambard was right – she had to reveal where the treasure was, even if it meant risking her own happiness.

She reached the corner of the field, climbed over the fence and set off down the road. It was narrow here and deserted. There were no treasure hunters in sight.

She walked around the next bend, deep in thought and not looking

where she was going. Hilton barked
a warning, but he was too late. She
bumped straight into Mr. Jackson from
the Clamerkin Historical Society. He
was on his hands and knees, examining
the path with Mrs. Damson.

"I'm sorry," said Amy.

"Don't worry," said Mr. Jackson as he climbed to his feet. "It's my fault entirely. I shouldn't be taking up so much room."

"And neither should I," said Mrs. Damson, who was kneeling beside him. "But we need to get down to ground level to search for clues." She took Mr. Jackson's outstretched hand and pulled herself upright.

"Tell them about the treasure," barked Hilton.

Amy hesitated. The feeling of being torn in two was even stronger now. It almost hurt.

Hilton barked again. "Go on – tell them now."

Amy gulped. Her mouth was so dry that she could barely speak. Was this a sign that she should stay quiet? Or was she just looking for an excuse not to risk revealing her secret?

Mrs. Damson didn't seem to notice Amy's dilemma. She just smiled and said, "I don't suppose you've remembered any more about that magpie."

Her words gave Amy the clue she needed. Suddenly a plan flooded into her mind – a plan that could reveal the whereabouts of the treasure without any risk at all.

"It's funny you should ask that," said Amy. "Because I've seen a magpie that looks just like that one."

"Oh!" shrieked Mrs. Damson. "It would be wonderful if you could point it out to us."

"It would fill me with *Joy* to do that," replied Amy. She spoke as loudly as she could, putting huge emphasis on the word Joy.

Luckily Hilton realized what she was trying to do. "Come here, Joy," he barked.

The magpie heard them both and flew onto a bush beside Mr. Jackson.

"There she is," said Amy, pointing at Joy. She winked at the magpie and added, "She must know where the treasure is. If you follow her, you might find it."

Joy winked back. Then she flew

off back the way they had come and landed on a holly bush.

Mr. Jackson tugged at Mrs. Damson's sleeve. "Come on. Let's follow that bird." Together they walked up to Joy.

The magpie waited until they had almost reached her. Then she pretended they had startled her, flew off again in the direction of the treasure and landed in a tree to wait until her pursuers had caught up. Then she repeated the whole process again and again.

"Joy's doing a great job," barked Hilton, as he and Amy followed the two adults.

"Shush," said Mrs. Damson, turning to Amy with her finger on her lips. "Don't let your dog frighten the bird away."

Amy knew there was no chance of that, but she pretended to quieten Hilton anyway. She didn't want to spoil the illusion that Joy had created so successfully. No one would have guessed she was deliberately leading the two adults in the direction she wanted.

Eventually they all reached the tree that marked the treasure's hiding place. As Mr. Jackson and Mrs. Damson approached, Webster dived underground and the rabbits scuttled under the hedge. But neither of the adults noticed them. They were concentrating too hard on the magpie.

Joy landed in front of the hole and started to peck at the grass as if that's why she was there. She hopped away as the two adults came closer, keeping up the pretense of being scared.

"There's a hole," cried Mrs. Damson. "It looks as if it's been dug by an animal."

Mr. Jackson had seen it too. He threw himself on the ground and pushed his arm inside. Then he gave a shout of triumph and pulled out the gold plate Amy had hidden there.

"Look!" he yelled, as he examined it carefully. "It's definitely Roman. I'm sure of that." Then he jumped to his feet and bounded up and down like Rascal, the baby rabbit. "We've done it," he cried. "We've found the treasure."

"It will take center stage in the Island Museum!" said Mrs. Damson, who looked just as excited but slightly less bouncy. Then she turned to Amy. "We can't thank you enough. Pointing out that magpie was exactly the help we needed."

And to Amy's delight, she didn't ask any awkward questions at all. The treasure hunt was over and the secret of the necklace was still safe.

Amy and Hilton left the adults admiring their find and slipped quietly away to the hedge. The magpie was already there. So were the cats and the rabbits.

"Thanks," she said to Joy. "You saved the day."

"No – you did," said Joy. "It was you who thought of the idea – I just made it happen."

"And what are you going to do next time you find a ring?" asked Willow.

"I'm going to leave it exactly where it is," Joy promised.

The End

❖ Amy Wild, ❖
❖ Animal Talker ❖

Collect all of Amy's fun, fur-filled adventures!

The Secret Necklace

Amy is thrilled to discover she can talk to animals!
But making friends is harder than she thought...

The Musical Mouse

There's a singing mouse at school! Can Amy find it
a new home before the principal catches it?

The Mystery Cat

Amy has to track down the owners of a playful orange
cat who's lost his home...and his memory.

The Great Sheep Race

Will Amy train the Island's sheep in time for her
school fair's big fundraiser – a Great Sheep Race?

The Furry Detectives

Things have been going missing on the Island and Amy
suspects there's an animal thief at work...

The Star-Struck Parrot

Amy gets to be an extra in a movie shot on the Island...
but can she help Plato the parrot land a part too?

The Lost Treasure

An ancient ring is discovered on the Island, sparking
a hunt for buried treasure...and causing chaos.

The Vanishing Cat

When one of the animals in the clan goes missing,
Amy faces her biggest mystery yet...